YET ANOTHER NASTY book

Suburb A tired man takes the last bus at night. He's the only passenger. He dozes in a back seat, and falls asleep. When he jerks awake, he realizes he's missed his stop.

Barry Yourgrau

Yet Another NASTY book

MiniNasties

Illustrations by Neil Swaab

JOANNA COTLER BOOKS
An Imprint of HarperCollins Publishers

He lives in a nice suburb, but the bus is careening along through the darkness of a desert!

Library of Congress Cataloging-in-Publication Data is available.
ISBN-10: 0-06-077676-5 (trade bdg.)
ISBN-13: 978-0-06-077676-3 (trade bdg.)

Typography by Neil Swaab
1 2 3 4 5 6 7 8 9 10
❖
First Edition

Frantically the man hurries up the aisle to the driver. He sputters out about his screwup.

To Anya, who keeps pleading, "Stop!"

The driver slowly turns around. The man gasps and staggers back. The driver's eyes are entirely white, like sinister eggs. He grins. He rises up out of his seat and comes lumbering

Contents

down the aisle, huge hands outstretched ahead of him to grab the man, who retreats, screaming, as the bus heaves along through darkness. The man trips, the driver seizes hold of him, starts shaking him. The man shrieks and struggles—and his eyes fly open.

"Mister, this is your stop!" The driver is speaking to him, from close above. He is

TUNES

A kid named Edgar fools around and accidentally swallows his cell phone.

How this happens is too complicated to explain here. The point is, Edgar's already late for school.

He rushes into the building. It's a place of enormous pressure. Students are warned not to waste precious seconds gabbing on cell phones—especially students with report-card "issues," like Edgar.

He sweats at his desk.

normal-eyed. Concerned. "You fell asleep," he says. "You were having a nightmare!" He

He prays for no calls, or for the cell-phone bat-
teries to have run out. No such luck. Horrified,
he hears the cute little ringing tune jingling away
in his stomach. His teacher and classmates hear
too. They stare. Desperately Edgar pretends he's
producing the tune himself. He grins, maneuver-
ing his lips.

"My new trick for Parents' Day," he gasps,
when there's silence at last. "Pretty cool, huh?"

No one agrees. The teacher frowns suspi-
ciously.

By lunchtime Edgar is a nervous wreck,
twisting his lips as call after call comes in.

Then the principal wants to see him.

Edgar stands trembling at the principal's big
desk. He blurts out the truth of his ludicrous and
irresponsible condition. He pleads for mercy,
promises to do extra assignments to make up for
any lost class time.

Right on cue, yet another call starts to jingle
away inside him.

"*Swallowed your cell phone,*" repeats the principal, scowling and baffled. "How on *earth* . . . ?"
He wheezes, peculiarly. "I mean, swallowing, say,

grins. "I recognized you from last week," he says. "Thank you, thank you so much," a *harmonica*, that I can understand. But a *cell phone?*"

The principal shakes his head. A tune toots up from his lips, exactly like a harmonica playing. And this functions as the painfully cute musical intro to what follows, when he suspends poor ringing-jingling Edgar on the spot.

mumbles the man. Embarrassed, he totters blinking off the bus, onto the street. For a

FANTASY RIDE

You ride the subway. It's packed. Misery oppresses you as the train careens and lurches. And then stops, for no good reason. Squashed in, you close your eyes and take refuge in fantasy.

When your eyes open, fantasy has come to life! To your amazement, the sweaty passengers clogged around you have all turned into monkeys. Chimpanzees, specifically! They squeal and screech in chimp-style frenzy, struggling in their silly suits and business blouses.

You hang on and laugh, in delight.

You squeeze your eyes shut again, again spring them open—another marvel!: A herd of

4

second his heart pounds as the bus drives away and he stares around where he is, in the commuter ostriches now are packed in around you. Bird heads bob idiotically on long necks! The train reaches a station and half the herd thunders away out the doors.

"What *joy*," you think. From here on, your ride to math tutoring will be your favorite part of the week. The train jerks from the station. And now inspiration lights a more tantalizing fire in your brain. Heart thumping, you close your eyes; and then peep out from the lids. The subway is crammed with commuters clad only in their underwear! Shrieks of modesty erupt. You gulp and squeeze your eyes shut, madly grinning, going for much, much more. Whereupon you reel, and give a loud *pop*, and turn into a frog on the floor.

"Dirty little beast!" hisses a nasty old commuter, giving you a kick with her shoe.

Because, unfortunately, she has her fantasy life too.

deserted lamplight, on the late-night street. But it's his nice suburb, just as he knows it.

Consumer Culture

Two goblins decide to go shopping in the big city. Everybody loves to shop, why not them?

However, being unfamiliar with modern consumer culture, the goblins just scowl back up at the clerk when she wants payment at the cash register. They aren't much at human-language skills either; the clerk finally loses patience with the two little bizarre men fiercely and dumbly clutching their nonsensical jumbles of bright things. Her impatience is understandable but unfortunate, since goblins are temperamental and (not widely known) they practice cannibalism. The clerk snarls something obviously

With a long sigh of relief, shaking his head, he starts home. Where the partner of the very rude; it's the last thing she ever says, apart from her screams.

The manager stalks over at the noise. He manages to shriek out the word, "Help!"

The security guard now comes huffing along, from his coffee break. He takes in the scene of carnage and consumerism, and immediately his mind starts working. He has aspirations to be a writer, you see; he scribbles away during his breaks. He's read about goblins. And now instead of squirting them in their teeny bristly eyes with pepper spray and clubbing them and calling the police, he makes signs that he'll let them go—on condition they later confide to him (somehow or other) their goblin life stories, which he will

7

monster who impersonated the real driver is waiting, white-eyed, for him.

turn into a sensational and remarkable book. They agree. But as they exit, the guard/writer unfortunately waves bye-bye, which is a very insulting gesture in goblin culture. So he loses his right hand, and his book. And all he gets in the end is a little story, written left-handed— very similar to this one.

Poor Gustave

A lad named Gustave
Says he must have

Another name.
Or he'll go insane!

But his name doesn't change,
It's too hard to arrange!

So poor Gustave's fate
Gets too sad to relate.

I'll just tell you he's gone
(Bonkers?)—that's all I'll say from now on.

Emily stares at her. Then she shrieks and runs out of the bathroom. She cowers back in bed under the blankets. After a good number of minutes, she gets up enough courage to creep back toward the bathroom. Heart pounding, she edges in just enough to glimpse the mirror. It's her own pale face that gapes back at her. The winking royal intruder is gone.

And she never returns.

But from that day on whenever Emily looks in her mirror, she can't help but wonder, a little forlornly, "Oh, why didn't I say yes? Oh, imagine being a princess! . . ."

*Hold up to the mirror to read
(if you dare!).

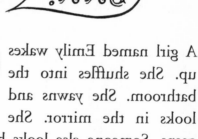

SHH!

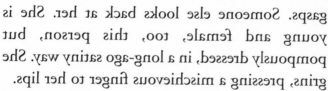

A girl named Emily wakes up. She shuffles into the bathroom. She yawns and looks in the mirror. She gasps. Someone else looks back at her. She is young and female, too, this person, but pompously dressed, in a long-ago satiny way. She grins, pressing a mischievous finger to her lips. "Shh!" she whispers from the mirror. "You mustn't be alarmed. They say I'm mad but I'm not. I'm only a princess who's tired of my silly royal life. And I want to exchange lives with you." She winks. "Okay?"

Encounter

Hello.

Hey, hi! What a nice surprise! Meeting you here.

Huh?

An unexpected treat—running into you.

But I live here. You're in my house.

This? Your house? I don't understand.

Why, someone told you somebody else lived here?

Yes. That guy told us—hey, where'd he disappear to?

You mean you're not alone? People came with you!

Sure. A whole busload. We're on an outing.

But this is crazy! Who gave permission for a bunch of strangers to invade my house?

I—gee, I don't know, I have to admit. But I do hope your word "strangers" doesn't apply to <u>me</u>.

Well, I happen to like you. But we've only met a couple of times before, really.

What? We've known each other, off and on, since first grade!

No we haven't!

Okay, now you're just messing with me!

Look, I don't know what all this is about, but I'd appreciate it if you rounded up the mob you came in here with and left, okay?

I'd be only too delighted, believe me. And I honestly have to say that you're one obnoxious kid.

And you, you're an ass, how's that?

Well then you're a jerk.

Creep.

Pajama-ed clown.

Delusional nitwit!

I curse the day I ever met you!

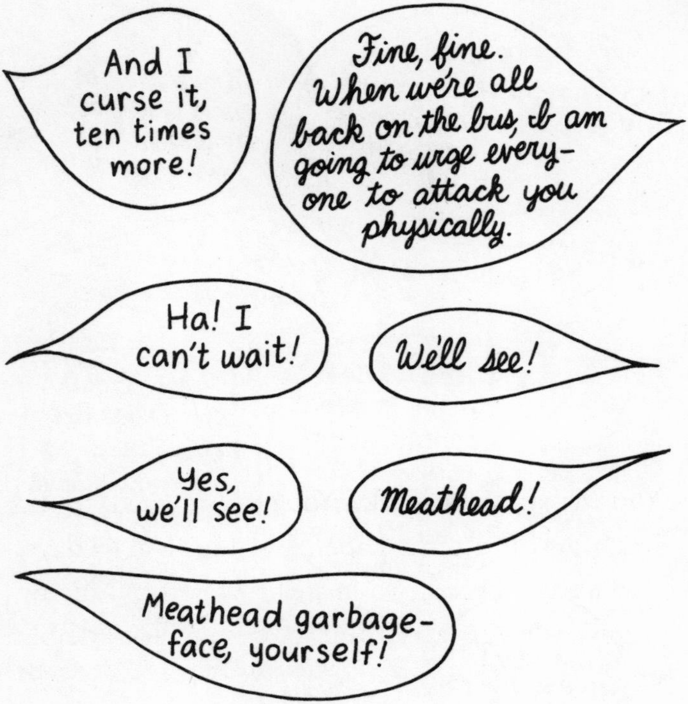
And I curse it, ten times more!
Fine, fine. When we're all back on the bus, I am going to urge everyone to attack you physically.
Ha! I can't wait!
We'll see!
Yes, we'll see!
Meathead!
Meathead garbage-face, yourself!

WIGGLE

You sit at your desk. You're supposed to be working on a term paper, it's due in two days. But you're bored. So instead you're practicing wiggling your ears. You've gotten remarkably good at this, being bored often.

Now today you feel in spectacular form, and you wiggle away earwise with all your might, as if your ears were actual hummingbird's wings. You hear the whirring of your efforts: To your amazement, you feel yourself start to lift, out of your chair, airborne, like some kind of Disney flying elephant! You gulp, straining away gleefully as hard as you're able, and you rise up, up over the desk, on toward the ceiling, ears wiggling and whirring. You squawk for joy, and this squawk breaks your focus, and violently you reel downward out of control, and crash across the table, sprawling headfirst onto the floor.

"What on earth?" shouts a voice from the other room.

It's your sister. She comes swaying through the doorway, upside-down. Astoundingly she supports herself on just the tips of two trembling fingers. "Aren't you supposed to be working on a term paper!" she demands.

Stunned from your fall, you struggle to manufacture an explanation. But your sister's screech interrupts. "Ow—my fingernail's breaking!" she cries. And a crucial digit gives way under her. She collapses full length into you. One of her descending shoe heels catches you right on the ear. And so for the rest of the week, your airborne days are over.

Maybe now you can get that term paper finished; but all this suggests why very little usually gets done at your house. And what does, takes forever and runs very short.

New World

A guy decides to invent nature. That's right: First he invents the tree. Then he invents the mustache, why not? Then he goes even further and invents hot chocolate.

After this he takes a break and just sits around for a while, drinking from his new mug and thinking things over.

When he gets back to work, it's with a splash. In one stroke he invents the whole line of portable things: portable TVs, DVD players, boom boxes; portable toilets for use during parades; portable plastic swimming pools for backyard fun.

And he confides to his friends his ultrasecret ambitions—the plans he's been hatching late at night in his notebooks—those pet projects of his inner vision that will dazzle the civilized world beyond its wildest dreams!

His friends smile faintly and stare down at their sneakers. They arrange a meeting among themselves; they're worried about the guy, very worried. They wonder if he isn't losing his marbles! They decide to seek out a wise counselor, for advice. The counselor doesn't exist quite yet, though, and they pace about anxiously, waiting for the guy to create him.

WHAT IS TRAGEDY?

You're thrown in jail for playing cards. This is in a grim age when all forms of amusement are forbidden. From your bleak cell bunk, you daydream of your pals sneaking from town to town with their bowling balls and their skateboards, amusing themselves stealthily under moonlit bridges, always on the lookout for the long shadow of the law.

Your days in jail go on and on. You make a few attempts at tic-tac-toe with your fingernail on the wall, but the guards are always watchful. So eventually you die of tedium. Your soul turns into a yellow parakeet. It pecks at the guards when they come in for your body. The guards squash it to death under their boots in a corner. The soul of the parakeet turns back into you. You dart out of the cell, lock the guards in, and deal yourself a hand of cards from the pack hidden all along in the heel of your boot.

You lose.

This is one of the two definitions of tragedy. The other one will really break your heart.

Right in the middle of her birthday party, Serena turns into a giraffe.

"Hope she's not expecting us to go out and buy all new presents!" mutter her friends, staring upward.

Friends can be like that, can't they.

Frogs

A girl wakes up. And screams. Her bed is covered with frogs.

There are frogs on the patterned rug, frogs on the dresser, frogs squatting on her computer—the new candy-colored laptop for her birthday!

The frogs croak. The girl shrieks. She leaps out of bed and lurches writhing out into the hall. More shrieks, more frogs! They crowd the hall carpeting, croak-croaking. The girl faints to the floor. The frogs hop onto her, their soft white throats pulsing in that creepy frog way.

They all wear little hats that say "Tori Weinstein for Student Council President."

Now more shrieking is heard—from the parents' bedroom. More frogs, frogs, frogs. Frogs downstairs in the living room, in the kitchen, way down in the basement, up on the shingles of the roof. In fact the whole neighborhood is jammed with pro–Tori Weinstein frogs.

All wearing their little campaign hats.

In one shadowy house down the street, set back a ways in the trees from its neighbors, a boy sits chuckling. He's actually a kind of wizard, this kid. But not Mr. Popularity, on account of his dopey looks (to be frank about them) and his know-it-all ways. And his social manner, which just seems to get things wrong all the time. He has had a big-time crush on Tori Weinstein for the whole school year. There's a banner, ELECT TORI WEINSTEIN, on his wall. He has gotten himself the unlikely job of being Tori's campaign manager.

"No other candidate has publicity anything like this," the boy wizard cackles, as he fastens more hats on the spellbound frogs around him. "Tori is gonna be thrilled!"

That's what he thinks.

HORSE
COSTUME

Your father comes home from work with a large package. He doesn't say anything. He goes up to his bedroom. When he comes back down he is wearing the hind section of a horse costume.

It's gray, with a large, stiff, brushlike tail that hangs down over his hooves as he walks sternly to the dinner table.

You turn wildly to your mother to say something, but she fixes you with a severe look. Disappointed, you take your seat. Your father eats his meat loaf and green beans in silence. You steal a glance at him between mouthfuls, until your mother kicks you in the ankle.

When he's finished, your father rises without a word and carries his empty plate into the kitchen. You hear him clump back out through the living room and up the stairs to his room. You swing around at last to your mother, but she just stares ahead grimly and you finish eating in silence. As you're washing up, she says simply: "There are certain things it's not for you to know."

That's all she says.

After you're in bed, you lie awake for a long time in the dark, unable to sleep. You listen to the sounds of horselike whinnying. You hear your mother's voice, low and anxious, pleading with your father.

"But it's not for me to know," you whisper to yourself.

And who's to say your mother isn't right?

PET

Young Otto keeps a pet, maybe you do too. But of all things, Otto's pet is a mosquito. One day, inevitably, the mosquito bites him. Otto reacts, inevitably, with a slap. So much for his pet.

Distraught, Otto buries the mosquito (what's left of it) in the backyard. But the grave is so tiny he can't find it again when he goes to visit a week later, with some flowers to leave in remembrance. Now Otto's truly distraught. He spends all weekend wandering from the back door to the garage and all along the fence, peering. Finally he goes out and extravagantly splurges all his young savings on flowers, which he scatters over the entire yard, in the hopes of randomly hitting the spot where his old pet is at rest.

Otto's mother watches all this from the kitchen window. She sighs, sourly. "Everybody else's kid has a normal regular-sized pet, like a dog," she mutters. "My Otto has to be the one with a minuscule bug! Where, oh where, does he get these crack-brained ideas?"

Shaking her head at her kooky offspring, she starts preparing dinner. She's making homemade ravioli tonight, so she gets out the microscope, to get started.

MY THREAT

A flea wants a talk show.
Don't laugh, 'cause even more so,

With his very first guest
He wants folks impressed

So he's going to ask . . . YOU
As his first guest (what can I do?).

Here's my word of advice:
Don't Scratch. Not even once (*never* twice).

If you scratch or itch he'll think you're mocking,
And he'll throw you off the show (how shocking).

And he'll have ME on instead
To read this lousy poem! (That's what he said.)

So get your itching over now,
And on the show stay stock-still, somehow.

(Or I *will* read this poem, so help me,
And the effect on us all will be deadly!)

CHICKEN NOODLE SOUP

For lunch, you order the chicken noodle soup special. Lunch progresses and you notice that your bowl of soup is not only sensational, value-wise, with big flavorsome chickeny chunks and thick noodles, it's also apparently inexhaustible. You spoon, slurp, burp, smile in pleasure—the level in the bowl stays the same!

You find this situation wonderful, but also eerie, even, well, alarming. The bowl should be empty by now, you should be full. But neither is so!

"I'm only supposed to take half an hour for lunch," you think, dazed. "But, boy, I have the *strangest* feeling I could sit here eating this marvelous bowl of soup (what a bargain!) all afternoon—all week. The whole month, even—even—*all year!*"

You giggle uneasily at this preposterous, perversely delicious thought.

From back in the kitchen, the cook peers stealthily out at you there at the counter. The cook is in fact a wizard. He has put all his ancient craft and art into your bowl of chicken noodle soup—which must keep its eater slurping away for three whole years, in order for the spell on the princess to be broken. The wizard loves the spellbound princess devotedly, he's known her since she was a baby child. So he watches you giggling and gulping your marvelous soup and he smiles, nodding slowly, determined to make this one *very* long lunch.

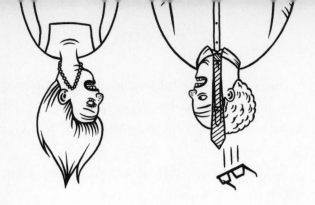

Fluffy Yellow

A teenage girl, Alyse by name, leaves her room to go down to breakfast. She acts strangely cautious. On the stairs, she gets a jolt.

Her parents are hanging upside down by their ankles from the front-hall ceiling, smeared from toe to nose with . . . fruit salad?

Alsye grunts and looks down at the fluffy yellow sweater she has on, and turns on her heel, shaking her head, and marches back to her room. She waits there, pursing her lips. She counts to sixty. She stares down at her fluffy yellow sweater again. She fingers it angrily. In determination, she strides out the door.

This time her mom and dad are dressed up like funny comic-book creatures and jammed headfirst through the stair banisters, as if victims of an explosion at a theme park.

"Darn this weird sweater!" Alyse mutters, stamping her foot.

Back in her room again she yanks off the colorful garment in question. She curses it and flings it in the corner. With a green jersey on instead, she exits and tramps downstairs. Everything perfectly normal now.

Her mother is at the stove as Alyse comes into the kitchen.

"Morning, hon," her mother says. And she then asks cheerily, "Hey, how come I never ever see you in that cute yellow sweater we got on vacation?"

"Oh, Mom—you wouldn't want to know," Alyse huffs.

Her mother blinks. She shakes her head over the eggs she's stirring. "Teenagers," she thinks. "They are so odd about clothes!"

33

A lonely guy, you know the type, dreams up a girl—his dream girl. He draws tender and adoring pictures of her, her and her immense brown eyes. He writes little stories in which he imagines the joys his beloved brings into his miserable life.

With shy pride he shares these documents of his heart's yearning with his one and only buddy.

This buddy immediately falls like a ton of bricks for what he sees.

He's a lonely guy too, and it's love at first

sight. Shyly, but with a joy he thought never to be his, he soon shows the first lonely guy his own fantasies of her, loveliest of lovelies: the dream girl. Who has left her creator and run off with her real true love—namely, himself.

"I hope you don't mind," he mumbles, awkward but shyly ecstatic.

Of course lonely guy #1 minds! "She's *my* dream girl!" he sputters, outraged. "Get your own!"

"She's mine now!" protests the smitten buddy. "She just *happened* to be 'yours' first by a laughable stupidity of fate!"

So their friendship ends on this bitter note. Each retreats to his dingy room in his parents' house and locks himself inside, consumed with invented romance: lonely guy #1 drawing and scribbling with tearful fury; his traitorous ex-buddy, with the airy bliss of a love thief.

This is what comes of loneliness, I guess.

As for the dream girl, the whole thing just bores her. But being a truly dependent type, she keeps her feelings to herself.

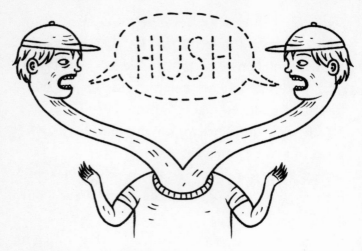

A boy blurts his crush
To a girl who says, "Hush.

Your words kind of scare me,
For nothing's prepared me

For a guy just like you!"
"Meaning (says he) my not one head but two?"

"Gee, I didn't notice," says she.
"It's your five knees that struck me!"

And she turns all red in the face—
As would you in her place!

Too Cute

A girl, let's call her Melanie, gets a pet—a pussy-cat. So adorable is this kitty, Melanie spoils it right from the start. Tender bits of salmon fill kitty's bowl; a satin pillow enhances kitty's sleeping basket.

Naturally all this goes to the animal's cute head and it starts to forget its place. It gets hold of Melanie's credit card somehow and starts splurging on silly but stupendously expensive little toys, mainly balls that glitter and jingle as they roll around while kitty gives chase.

Melanie turns pale at her credit-card bill. Angrily she confronts her out-of-control pet, who first acts all huffy—then goes into its little routine, meowing so poignantly, blinking big pussycat eyes, quivering its pretty whiskers.

Melanie is powerless to resist such cuteness.

She takes a second job to pay off her credit-card debts, and when she's fired from both, because of sleepiness, she falls to begging in the streets. All to keep the adorable little beast happy with more colorful balls to go hunting under the sofa!

And then one day pretty kitty chases one of its purchases outside the door, onto the street, and gets run over flat by a car.

Melanie is grief-stricken, of course. But you'd hope this terrible shock might turn out for the best, by removing the spoiled monster of cuteness from her life.

But not so. Melanie just wastes away, clutching kitty's breathtakingly expensive playthings to her chest as she expires from a broken heart!

This is what happens sometimes. Which is why, if I were you, I'd think very carefully about getting myself a pussycat.

Thin Air

A bored magician has a lapse in concentration during his magic show and, by accident, makes his entire audience disappear.

And he can't bring them back. They're gone, into thin air.

In a panic he scurries back to his hotel.

"So, how'd the show go?" asks the desk clerk.

"Fine, fine," mumbles the magician. He rushes upstairs, then suddenly rushes back down and makes the clerk disappear too. Just to get rid of witnesses.

Then he drives out of town, fast.

Ten miles away, suddenly he pulls over, turns

around wildly, and heads back. By brain-exhausting magical effort he makes the whole town disappear!

Then he heads away, stunned at what one lapse in concentration has led to.

The magician drives for days. At first there's no news of his crimes. Then the world finally realizes something's gone. Headlines blare:

Have You Seen This Town?

And: **What Monster Stole Sunnyville, California?**

"*Monster . . .*" whispers the magician. What worse names will they use when they find him? Oh, why'd he ever do a show in dull, dim little Sunnyville!

For a feverish afternoon he considers making the entire state of California disappear. But where will it all end?

There's only one solution. He writes a con-
fession, begging forgiveness. Then he takes the
coward's way out and makes himself disappear
too.

But because of his emotional state, he has a
lapse in concentration and one of his ears and a
thumb remain behind, visible.

Believe it or not, the authorities are so furious, they put the ear and thumb on trial! And
then they lock them away, in a dull, dim little jail
cell, forever.

CHOCOLATE MINT

A kid—not you I hope—gets an ice-cream cone: strawberry swirl. He takes a bite; he drops the cone and grabs his mouth.

"This's boiling hot!" he sputters.

The clerk grins. "Joke's on you!" he cries. He laughs wildly, like a clown. In fact he looks like a clown: frizzy red hair, big red lips, red cheeks.

"Welcome to the circus!!" cries the clown.

To great applause from an audience that's suddenly all around, the clown leaps over the ice-cream counter and grabs the startled kid.

"Hey!"—the kid protests, as the clown folds him up, head between legs, and stuffs him down the mouth of a big black cannon.

"Put your fingers in your ears or you'll go deaf!" the clown whispers. The kid frantically manages to, just before a thunderous roar sends him flying into the air, to spectacular applause, up toward a hole in a tent roof—up and out into the sky.

"H-h-help!"—the kid cries, perceiving no means to get back down.

The clown suddenly appears nearby in midair. A propeller whirs on the little helmet he wears.

"Thanks for being a good sport!" he shouts merrily. "Afraid you're on your own from here. But come in and have a free scoop of chocolate mint, if you make it back alive!"

And he laughs and toots a rubber-bulb horn. He whizzes away down toward the tent below.

"B-but—I don't like *chocolate*

mint!" the kid protests, as he plunges now out of control toward the ground.

But the clown is already in the distance, zipping along under his propeller, laughing, squawking his horn.

And my question is: How can anybody not like chocolate mint?

A Bad Case

A man (like your uncle, maybe?) has a bad cold. He tries to get rid of it by eating lots of raw garlic and onions. His breath becomes stupendously obnoxious. You can imagine!

He loses his job (his office mates refuse to come near him) and is forced to move in to a room in someone's house (he's not married), to save money. He spends most of his time up in his room, taking his meals there because his landlady can't stand the smell of his breath and his food. His cold has been long gone, but he has become addicted to "g&o." He has bags of the stuff under his bed, boxes stacked in the closet. One day he hits on the idea of writing a book of poems about his beloved edibles. The project would give him something to do and maybe bring in a little money; who knows? He works away excitedly for a bit. But he really never has been good at this sort of thing; after a while his attention just sort of drifts away.

Finally he takes to just sitting up in his room, looking over at what's to eat, then staring vacantly out the window at the world. Every time he lets out a breath, a horrid little stink spreads into the room.

Boy, aren't you glad you're not there with him!

"Doogie's the Man!"

A boy named Doogie discovers an amazing magic formula which enables him to skip school whenever he wants, without anyone noticing, to star in his own hit TV show, "Doogie's *the Man*!"

Unfortunately at this point his alarm goes off and he wakes up.

A silly vampire
Suddenly feels *old*,
Which is reasonable.
Vampires are *ancient*, I'm told.

But this silly vampire
Has a goofy idea:
He's got into his fanged head

That he's a *teen* monster (don't sneer).

"Oh, please, it's so *awful*
Not feeling *young* anymore!"

These are his words to a shrink

After he's burst in and locked the door.

The shrink takes one look

At those vampirish fangs,

And sees right away, cleverly,

Where his security hangs.

"*You?* Why, you're a *y-young un*!
That's plain as day—I mean night!
Your being *old?* What a *joke—hah hah hah—*
And a *bad* one, all right!"

"*Gee, really??*" cries the vampire,
With a big wrinkly grin.
And he grabs the shrink to kiss him
("No—wait!" the shrink sputters—)
And, oops, his vampire teeth sink in.

"*Oooops,*" goes the silly gory ghoul,
As he sucks out the shrink's blood.
"But what the heck, I'm *YOUNG*!
Say it loud! Say it proud!"

(And the shrink, he says nothing.
Clever? No: just, you know,
all out of, like, blood.)

49

A dog is gobbling its breakfast when suddenly it realizes it can see into the future. It sees something terrible happening to itself, very shortly.

Frantically the dog rushes upstairs into the bathroom. Its owner is in the tub.

"You gotta help me, something terrible's going to happen to me!" cries the dog. But of course all its master understands is a lot of crazy barking and yapping and spraying of bits of dog food.

"Get out of here, you lunatic mutt!" the owner shouts. "Can't you see I'm taking a bath?"

This lack of comprehension makes the dog

even more frantic. It howls and claws at the tub, and its owner gets so mad he comes roaring out of the water and hauls the protesting animal downstairs by its collar.

"And stay out, you nutball!" he cries, shoving the dog out the door, which he then slams.

This is what the dog gets for trying to communicate its terrible near future that it's miraculously been able to glimpse.

For a while it scratches pitifully at the door, pleading. Then slowly it turns and goes whimpering away down the street, to meet its fate. An elderly motorist has a sneezing fit right then and loses control, and the dog squeezes its eyes shut, waiting to be run over. And it is.

The dog's ghost returns home that night. Its master sits in his armchair, sniffing his tears. At heart he loved that dopey mutt. "See, I told you what would happen!" the canine ghost tells him, laying on the guilt.

But of course, the owner comprehends not a word of what the dog is saying.

shampoo

You're absorbed in an awkward attempt at cutting your fingernails, when you hear your friend's cries of help from her bathroom. Not so much cries as squeaks.

"God, what *now?*" you think. You just stopped by for a quick visit.

You find her flapping helpless at the bottom of her tub. She has shrunk to the size of a rodent; her hair is sudsy with shampoo.

"Will you stop wasting money on insanely expensive shampoos with all these weird side effects!" you lecture her, drying her off and

carrying her in a towel into her bedroom.

"I'm fine," she squeaks defen-
sively. "It only lasts an hour, it's wonderful for
my hair. Just don't sit on me."

"You think shrinking to the size of a gerbil is
healthy?" you snarl. "Or last month, when you
spent *sixty dollars* on hair gel that made you swell
so big you couldn't get through the door for two
days, and your clothes wouldn't fit for a week—
that's fine and dandy with you?" you demand.

"Look who's talking!" she squeaks back.
"What about those disgusting cheapo cosmetics
you buy, that shampoo—you think it's *healthy*
having a bunch of fingers growing out of
your scalp!"

"I told you, the drugstore says they'll all
fall out in a couple of days," you
retort. "And my case doesn't change
yours! What's more, I'm now able to give
myself a stimulating scalp massage
regardless of what else I'm doing." And you
demonstrate, causing your friend to squeal again

53

in horror. You flap all sets of fingers at her, in annoyance.

And so you return to your nail clipping, which we now can fully appreciate for the awkward labor that it is.

Iron Tree

Two no-good squirrels kid-nap a grandmother during her nap. How they're able to is a mystery. But they do it.

They stuff sleeping grandmother into a hole in a tree deep in the park, without waking her.

Then they scramble into the branches to watch their cruel practical joke unfold.

Granny finally stirs, and squawks, and bangs her gray head, sitting up. The squirrels snicker and twitch their tails in no-good pleasure. They twitch more as granny, poor old thing, tries to squeeze out of the tree, and does, and falls in the dirt. And then struggles up and peers about, confused whether she's still napping and this is all a bad dream.

Alas, no.

The squirrels hop along their branch to watch granny totter off calling, "He-e-lp!" weakly, to find a way home. The squirrels raise paws and give a squirrelly high-five.

They should pay attention.

Down below another wrinkled old lady watches. She's a witch. She was wandering through the park, collecting worms and spiders for her cauldron. And she's seen the whole cruel practical joke with her pitch-black eyes.

She's waited for granny

to get clear of the tree.
Now she hurries to it,
chanting a spell.

The tree shudders and
rattles—and turns into iron.

The squirrels squeak in
alarm. The witch chants,
and flames leap in the tree
hole. The iron tree slowly
turns red-hot, foot by foot.

The squirrels squeal on
their heating branch. They
try to spring away—but
they're stuck fast by the
spell. They shriek, poor
suffering things. Their tails
begin to smoke!

The witch grins at the
sight. So does granny,
who's come back, hearing
the shrieking. And the two
gnarled little old ladies
exchange a nice, wrinkly,
nasty high-five.

BUBBLE TROUBLE

A kid, Clarence by name, blows a bubble-gum bubble. Kids and gum: an age-old combo. And this gum is a brand-new, super-bubble bubble gum. A guy in a funny pink cap is giving away samples by a park in the sunshine.

Clarence blows, and his super-bubble bubble swells big. Then bigger—then enormous. Slowly Clarence lifts off the ground and rises into the air! He giggles in disbelief through the puffing O of his mouth, rising on up past the treetops! Sure, a healthy twinge of fear goes through him as he floats away into the blue—fear at what's going to happen when his bubble bursts.

But he's clever, this Clarence. He's managed to sneak extra gum samples. He has a whole pocketful of them! He grips several in readiness, set to shove them in his mouth and chew-chew and blow-blow, when the spectacularly stretched one-sample bubble he's attached to goes *pop!*

Back down below by the park, the guy in the pink cap gives away the last of his gum samples and hurries off. He's grinning, thinking of the little pile of money he's made for himself, having sneakily switched old gum samples with most of the brand-new ones, which he'll sell at a nice price. All that old gum was perfectly fine— so what if it isn't "super-bubble"?

So let's just keep our fingers crossed for clever Clarence, way up there, shall we?

Fairy Tale

Two boys play all alone near the big high house in the countryside. It's afternoon. Their yells and breathless cries are the only noise in the landscape. Their games bring them at last indoors, away from the wide trees and the chairs on the lawn. They rush about the empty house: doors slam, closets bang. They're playing hide-and-seek now. One of the boys, the one who lives in the house, scurries upstairs, pausing at each floor to look back over his shoulder, giggling with nervousness, as he makes his way to the attic.

He scampers to a place under the low, sloped

ceiling and crouches there in the shadows, behind some boxes and a chest of drawers piled with dusty books. He peers around the boxes, eyes riveted on the top of the stairs, hands to his mouth to cover his suspense, to see if his new pal will discover where he is.

Behind him, beyond his shoulder, from deep in the dusty dimness comes an almost noiseless patter of clawed feet. The boy doesn't hear it, his eyes on the stairs. The wolf has come up the back way. It slips forward stealthily through the shadows. It has removed the stocking cap and wig, the cool jacket with the logo, the orange sneakers. Its pale eyes are glittering.

Knock

Knock

"Hello? Who is it?"

"Hello. Sorry to bother you, it's your neighbor. Is everything all right?"

"Who? It's two a.m.!"

"Your neighbor. I'm sorry, I'm sure I heard screams. Is everything all right?"

"No one screamed here. I don't know what you're talking about."

"Are you sure? I heard a lot of screaming. Perhaps you should open this door."

"I'm not opening the door! Everything's fine, I tell you. I was sound asleep, for heaven's sake, you woke me up, it's two a.m. No one was screaming here—*everything's fine.*"

"I'm—I'm sorry . . . but are you sure? I'm certain
I heard screams. Definitely screams."

"No one was screaming here, can't you understand? Go away, okay?"

"I'm afraid I can't. You just—you just never know these days. Please unlock this door."

"No! I'm not unlocking the door! There were no screams! What do you want, you weirdo? *There were no screams.*"

"Well, there will be."

"What?"

"Oh, never mind, I'll let myself in." (Laughs).
"Well, here I am behind you, that was easy.
Should have thought of it before. Hey, cool paja-
mas, may I feel the—" (Laughs again.) "See?
Now I told you there'd be a lot of screaming,
didn't I?"

STEPHEN KING, CHEERS!

After a night of making merry, Ira loses his way home. He finds himself deep in a forest. He blinks at dark trunks and boughs, at shadowy leaves and thickets. "Hey," he hiccups. "I live in a densely populated city! What's this?"

His heart hammers. Something wriggles in the bushes nearby, and he yelps and scuttles behind a tree. He peeps from there, like a coward in a comedy skit.

Silence reigns but for the noise of his heart. After a while, Ira forces his cowardly self to start searching for a way out. He sways off on a vague faint path, moaning, cursing. Black branches scratch his cheeks and neck. His heart keeps hammering, so his pace speeds up with it. Another wriggling rustling close by sends him floundering at full gallop through the greenery, screaming.

In this manner Ira bursts onto a street corner, and finally halts, gasping, by an all-night grocery. He stands doubled over, panting, shaking like a leaf.

He stares back where he's escaped from . . . and sees only darkened buildings, windows! He gapes in bewilderment. He staggers into the grocery and comes back out no wiser, now ashamed by the smirks he got for an answer. He stares again; no forest anywhere.

Under these circumstances Ira finally reaches the safety of his front door, and his familiar bed. After he turns out the light he sits up for a long time, pondering. He shakes his head. He swears off too much fun and late nights, for keeps! Mystified still, he sinks at last onto his cozy pillow, under his cozy blanket, and loses himself in sleep.

But something wakes him . . . that *rustling* from the bushes. . . .

It's now beside him on the carpet.

Thoughtful Ghost

Young Winston sees a ghost one night and is so shocked by the sight (who wouldn't be?), he loses all power of speech. He communicates with the world (when he does) by means of little notes he scrawls pathetically on bits of paper his mother collects for him.

Mostly he just sits in his room, twitching at the wall, shuddering at the memory of what he saw when he peered in through the broken window of the old abandoned house, under the full moon, beyond the NO TRESPASSING sign.

For its part, the ghost feels bad too. It remembers poor Winston's look of petrified terror when it shook its greenish decaying arms at him, when it wailed with its gaping maggot-infested mouth—really just being playful, to give Winston a little scare, to reprimand him for trespassing.

But now it wonders if it overdid things, perhaps.

And alas for shivering Winston, and his future as a functioning human being, the ghost decides to go along and find him, wherever he is, and express its thoughtful apologies in person.

HOMEWORK

A girl with much homework
Says, "Why won't this phone work!?

'Cause I gotta get help
For my bio and math!"

(That doesn't rhyme, but so what?
It's all the rhyme that I got.)

But the phone doesn't function
And for the girl that's the junction

Where her school year turns so lousy,
She's thrown out of her house-y.

(And if my rhyme is a howler,
The girl's view of phones is much fouler!)

MORE HOMEWORK

It's the end of the school day. Kids should be pouring out of the building, shouting and laughing. They should be hurrying off to soccer, or biking over to a friend's place to rehearse in a cool crude rock band. They should be buzzing along on skateboards, they should be—

Instead they come trudging out, heads sunk, all groaning like prisoners shuffling to their doom. Dark shadows ring their dull eyes, young backs are bent like old people's—from ceaseless hours hunched over books. A air of hopeless suffering hangs over them:

The suffering of endless, crushing *homework*.

Up in the teachers' lounge a thin sinister figure—a math teacher—rubs his bony hands.

"Look at 'em all . . . *suffering*," he murmurs gleefully.

Beside him at the window watches a fat sly person who resembles a nasty pig that got indoors by wearing a wig. She teaches literature. "How much you load 'em with tonight?" she grunts excitedly.

"Tons of terrible algebra!" chuckles the spindly math teacher. "Tons and tons of torturous equations and formulas! You?"

"Ooh, essays!" grunts the piggy lit teacher. "Essays and more essays about the most boring, complicated, useless poems ever written!" She cackles in pleasure.

The other teachers in the lounge all cackle too. They gaze down at the sad kids slumping along in the sunshine below.

"Yeah, ain't it grand how miserable we can make 'em!" chuckles a history instructor, who has a large wart on the

THE
UNBEARABLE
LIGHTNESS
OF BEING IN
SCHOOL

tip of his nose. He scratches it with his fat fingers and he snorts, repulsively and happily.

But of course this whole scene is imaginary. It's all a joke. Everybody knows this isn't the real story behind homework! Am I right? Why of course I am.

NOISY

Your neighbor below is blasting music. You're all for loud music—but not right now. You need to take a nap, you got up really early even though it's Sunday. Finally you bang on the floor with a broom handle, in protest.

"Creep!" a snotty teen voice shouts up at you through the floorboards.

Creep?

In a fury you stamp downstairs to the deafening door underneath you. There you freeze in bewilderment. All is silent. "Huh?" you say. You press your ear close. Through the door you can hear the soft twittering of birds . . . the soothing lilt of a harp. A voice is tenderly . . . humming?

Back in your apartment, the decibels continue to throb! You rush about ratlike, ear to one wall, then another; you flop down on your knees and listen pathetically through the floorboards. *That's where it's coming from!*

Furious, you pound again.

"Quit it, creep!" the snotty voice shouts up.

"*You* quit it—*creep double creep!*" you shriek back, your nap-yearning nerves starting to unravel. You pound and pound with the broom.

You rush back downstairs. The softly lilting door is . . . still softly lilting. You stare at it. After much hesitation, you knock, timidly.

"Who is it?" a sweet, elderly voice calls.

"It's—um, listen, um—oh never mind," you say.

"Who?"

"Never mind," you repeat. "Sorry!"

You droop back upstairs. You huddle in your tiny bedroom, fingers in your ears, your despair bitter with confusion as waves of mystifying noise engulf you from below.

"But how—*how* can something so tormenting,

so unexplainable, so strange be happening!" you plead aloud.

What a question, for anybody who lives in an apartment!

Sha^mE

A superbrainy young man who styles himself *Jerry.GO²* makes a sensational invention. It's a handheld gadget that scientifically removes the feeling of "shame" from a person!

The social implications of this invention are awesome. The financial implications for its young inventor? Dazzling, to say the least!

So dazzled is brainy *Jerry.GO²* by his visions of riches that he forgets to watch his step getting off the bus with his invaluable invention in hand, on his way to the manufacturer he's secretly contacted. And he trips. The marvelous gadget flies out of his hand into the street. The bus departs right over it, *crunch*.

If ever there was a time to feel the crippling weight of "shame" about a piece of stupidity, this would be it. But luckily the young inventor has personally tested his gadget on himself. "Oh well," shrugs *Jerry.GO²*, shamelessly. "I'm brainy, I'll just make another one!"

But before that he decides to invent a gadget to remove "forgetfulness"—to guard against any unnecessary repeats of not watching his step, etc. This gadget however proves unexpectedly tricky to make. So, brainily, *Jerry.GO²* decides to invent first a device that *implants* "total forgetfulness"— from which he'll then reverse engineer his fool-proof "anti-forgetfulness" model. This tactic starts out like a charm. He tests the *implant* version on herself, with flying colors!

Which is why you can forget about ever seeing that "anti-shame" gadget, I'm ashamed to say.

Lunch

A girl is so busy at the library office where she volunteers Saturdays, so hardworking, she doesn't have time to go to lunch. But she's starving! Finally she just has to eat something—she takes a bite of her pencil. It tastes . . . *good*. Splintery, but surprisingly good! Delighted, the girl tries a crunchy chew of a colored pen. Another pleasant surprise! With relish she quickly polishes off two noisy packages of pencils and colored pens. She smacks her lips and starts on the Major Overdues notebook. Delicious! But the more she eats, the hungrier she feels. It must be the chemicals she's downing, god knows. She jumps to her feet, grabs her folding chair, and wolfs that down. Then the desk she shares—then the filing cabinets! Then every stick of furniture throughout the office, *munch munch*, the potted plants, the Xerox copier, the telephones—all three computers left unattended by her coworkers, who are all out for a leisurely lunch.

Finally the girl stops, wipes her lips, and lets out a long breath. She pats her belly. She gives a loud burp. She giggles. And since there's no more work to be done now because there's no more library office left, she puts on her coat and heads home early.

End of the pretzel

"Hi, I just wanted to come over, man, and tell you, you're amazingly talented!"

"Thank you. . . . That's . . . very kind."

"No, I mean it. I been watching you almost an hour! Hey—doesn't it hurt?"

"Actually, it does. Very much, actually."

"Thought so. I mean, I seen people put their ankles behind their head and all—but wow, you're all twisted and wrapped up with yourself. Like a pretzel!"

"That's what they call me: the Human . . . Pretzel."

"I hear ya. That's good, that's good!"

"Thanks. Listen, do me . . . a small . . . favor?"

"Sure, man. Just say it!"

"Please call 911 . . . again. The ambulance should have come . . . forty-five minutes ago. . . ."

"Forty-five minutes? That's awful, man, that's tragic!"

"Yeah."

"I'll call, absolutely! Gee, you look pretty weird in the face. Almost purple."

"I know. I'm . . . suffocating."

"Oh, wow! Yeah, yeah. Hey, look, can I like, help, like, untangle you?"

"No, that would probably . . . kill me. Listen, will you call them?"

"Sure, sure, right away! But I don't have a cell phone."

"There's one . . . in my pocket."

"Which pocket, man?"

"That one. . . ."

"Oh, gee. Oh, gosh, it's not going to be easy, man, getting at it there!"

"Please . . . help. . . . Hurry . . ."

"Oh man, oh man. I'll try! . . . Oops—sorry,

man, didn't mean to tickle you, told you it wouldn't be—gee, don't giggle like that, man! Please, you're gonna—oh my god, no! *Don't laugh*! No, stop, man, your—oh no, don't— *don't*!"

Houndstooth

A girl named Keri, so cool and full of fun you'd want her for your friend, suddenly becomes ill. She lies in bed wasting away. Ominous black-and-white patterned marks appear on her skin. The terrible diagnosis is made: *houndstooth-check poisoning.*

"More than others, Keri went overboard for this new craze for houndstooth," murmurs the doctor. "And it will cost her her young life." He shows her distraught parents the X-rays: houndstooth has invaded Keri's bodily tissues, her vital inner organs; soon even her lovely big blue eyeballs will be houndstooth! Her parents clutch each other, wailing.

At home the tragic girl sighs through her houndstooth-checked lips, on her houndstooth pillow, under her houndstooth sheets, by her houndstooth-papered wall, under her houndstooth-decorated ceiling. Houndstooth curtains stir in the window, trendy in their deadly way. Keri's friends gather around her bed, somber at the fate of one who will die simply from being so devoted to style.

"But the silly thing is, houndstooth isn't really cool anymore!" mutters a buddy of Keri's younger brother, who happens to be visiting. This remark provokes outrage. The buddy is forced to apologize, before being banished from the room.

But he knows he's right. *Corduroy* is the new coolest thing, just ask him. Or go after him and pry a look under the big bandage on his neck—where the first fatal corduroy markings have already appeared.

Pickled Peppermint-Pineapple Soda

For fun, an evil spirit takes up residence in a vending machine on the street. A couple of teenagers come hurrying along at night and shove in their money for cans of the supernew trial brand of pickled peppermint-pineapple soda—and begin shouting and cursing when no cans come out. This is the evil spirit's idea of a little joke.

Unaware of what they're dealing with, the furious teens begin kicking and slapping the machine, rocking and wrenching it from side to side. All of which makes the evil spirit seasick. Whereupon the vending machine starts viciously blasting out soda cans at its abusers, like an artillery barrage. The shocked battered teens yell and scramble back despite the freebies, and then run off shrieking in terror as the vending machine unbelievably gives chase, inclining at an aggressive angle, bombarding away.

At last the street is silent, empty but for cans scattered like rubble in the moonlight, and the vending machine marooned halfway down the block. The evil spirit decides this is all boring and annoying, really, and it moves on elsewhere.

And so this strange episode comes to an end. Draw from it what lesson you wish. The makers of pickled peppermint-pineapple soda take perhaps the wrong lesson and decide their new trial product provokes such an unexpectedly violent reaction that it can't be safely introduced. Which is why you've never had a taste of it, now, have you?

Something

He

Ate?

A guy (friend of your dad's?) comes home from dining at a restaurant and discovers that all his teeth are missing. They must have somehow got taken away when the dishes were being cleared. They're perfectly fine healthy teeth, he takes good care of them.

He starts to telephone the restaurant; but then he feels embarrassed, phoning about this. He calls a taxi instead and heads back to the restaurant in person. He wears a scarf wound around his

sniff.
sniff.

face, to hide his absurdly sunken lips. As the taxi pulls up to the restaurant, he rearranges the scarf a final time. To his horror, he now finds himself holding his nose and one of his cheeks in his hands. He appears to be falling apart! Maybe it was something he ate?

"I've changed my mind," he blurts out to the taxi driver. "Take me home!"

By the time the taxi pulls up back at his house, he is essentially a bunch of parts he's frantically clutching together. "Please, help me get inside!" he manages to blurt out, with a burp of the monstrous meal probably responsible for this living nightmare.

"You bet!" cries the young taxi driver, and he leaps out to give a hand. It's his first night on the job, he wants to make a good impression. He finds another line of work in a hurry, that's for sure.

Pass the Salt

A fat old king falls down dead.
His young wife says, "Yummy!"
—And bites off his head.

She wolfs it right down, and gives out a burp;
And then starts on his fingers
With a snort and a slurp.

His ankles, his toes, his liver and stomach:
All go down the gullet
Of the gobbling gal monarch!

At last someone creeps forward, trembling
And quiet, and timidly whispers,
"Uh, perhaps Your Highness should diet?"

"I would if I could!" the queenly gnosher replies.
"But it's not all that often
One's tasty hubby dies!

And royal flesh is so *scrumptious*, who can resist?
So pass the salt, will ya?
And we can both share his left wrist!"

INCONVENIENCE

The bus stops. A mom (like yours?) gets off. She trudges up the block, weighed down by a bag of groceries. When she arrives at her apartment building, she sets the bag down outside. She sighs mightily and reaches into the bag.

She brings out four large suction cups. She straps two cups on her knees, and slings the grocery bag over her shoulder, backpack-style. Then she fits her hands into the straps of the other two cups.

Grimly, she starts climbing.

At the fourth floor, she needs a rest. She

swings the bag onto an air conditioner, and takes a great lung-filling breath. She looks around at the view high above the street. Carelessly she leans out too far and the hiss of air releasing from the suction cups shocks her ears. She scrambles wildly, horribly, grabbing on to the air conditioner.

She curses, heart hammering. She waits to calm down. Then she resets the suction cups, swings the bag back on, grits her teeth, and starts on up the wall.

At last she reaches the ninth floor. She heaves the groceries through the open window and struggles over the sill. Inside, she stands panting. She unstraps the cups, dropping them noisily on the floor. She picks up the groceries.

"Anybody home?" she calls, trudging toward the kitchen.

Her husband appears in the kitchen doorway.

"Hi," he says, turning sideways to let her by. "Look what those straps did to my hands just now," he says, holding up the damage.

Your mother shakes her sweaty head as she lifts the groceries onto the counter.

"What I'd like to know," she declares, "is how long can it take to fix one lousy elevator!"

Blossoms

A girl discovers a
blossom growing out
of the side of her head.
She touches it in disbelief.
She tries to wiggle it off, but it
hurts. So she stops. In the
drowsy moonlight of her bed-
room, the blossom's scarlet petals nod out
through her hairdo. And then they start to swell,
heavily, pulling her head over to the side. The
girl flaps and struggles to her feet, but her cries
are muffled by the sudden green embrace of an
encircling vine. More vines topple the girl onto

her bed. A carpet of gorgeous flora swarms over her, drowning her pajamaed figure in a swarming riot of growth and scent, there in the moonlight of her bedroom.

This is the daydream of a young florist, dozing in his flower shop. The girl is a customer of his. Next time she comes in, he works up the courage to shyly present her with a lovely red rose, for free. But she just looks at him, and sniffs, and says, "No thank you."

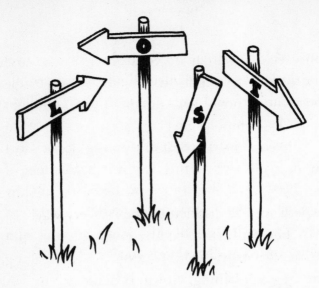

"Pardon me, can you help me? I'm a little lost."

"I'm sorry. I'm lost too!"

"Of course—how selfish of me! Everyone must feel lost. It's all very disorienting."

"Yes. You'd think the city authorities would have more sense than to rearrange all the streets in town, with only an hour's warning to anyone!"

"It's almost absurd, isn't it? And imagine what it must cost, all the equipment involved, all the workers who toil away frantically tearing up the paving and then reassembling it god knows where else."

"Honestly, it's practically a scandal. I was

only able yesterday to locate my house, after months of looking for it after the *last* rearrangement—and now I have no idea where it can be!"

"Oh, you poor guy!"

"Excuse me, I'm a sixty-three-year old grandmother!"

"Oh, pardon me, pardon me. This whole experience has disoriented me in every way!"

"That's all right, I understand, no need apologize. Honestly! Well, I guess I'll hobble along, no use complaining. Got to be patient."

"That's right. Be patient! Well, good luck, buddy—I mean, grandmother, pardon!"

"Really, it's all right. And good luck to you too. Good luck to us all!"

A kid hurries down into the street. He's all out of sugar for his breakfast cocoa. He likes it

extrasweet, he's a "two spoonfuls more" man,
and he's already fixed a steamy mugful, it's back

there waiting for him, losing precious heat. So he starts to run.

He speeds along in the morning sunshine. And just like that he becomes airborne—for five full seconds he floats, like a bubble, three feet off the ground! Then just like that he's back to earth.

He staggers, and reels on. He buys his sugar at the corner store in a state of amazement.

This airy miracle never occurs again. For a while the kid runs, he runs everywhere. Faster,

faster! But all he gets is tired. Days pass. Life resumes as before, normal and earthbound, with this one unaccountable dreamlike outburst there in its midst—as if a golden tower from a fairy tale had thrust up for a moment in a dull river as the kid drifted by.

The kid ponders this mystery of his every morning. He shakes his head, he sips his

extrasweet cocoa. He has no explanation, and
nor do I. And I wonder, what little mystery do

you shake your head at, you yourself? As you sit
there in the early morning sunlight, so normal,

so familiar. And you ponder, and sip, and bump
softly against your kitchen ceiling.

BAD MANGA

A MOUSE READS SOME MANGA LEFT OPEN ON THE KITCHEN TABLE. INSPIRED, IT DECIDES TO BECOME A SUPERHERO.

"SURE, I MAY SEEM AN INSIGNIFICANT LITTLE RODENT," IT THINKS, IN THE DARKNESS OF ITS MOUSE HOLE BEHIND THE STOVE. "BUT IN REALITY I'M **LovingMouse** — CHAMPION OF PEACE BETWEEN GUYS AND GIRLS!"

THE MOUSE HAS DECIDED IT WILL BE THE HEROIC AGENT WHO FINALLY RESOLVES THE AGE-OLD DIFFICULTIES BETWEEN THE SEXES!

AND IT FASHIONS ITSELF A CUTE LOVINGMOUSE CAP, TO PLAY THE PART, ALONG WITH A SCRAP OF DISCARDED SOCK AS A CAPE. TO LAUNCH ITS CAREER, IT WAITS TO HEAR THE BOYFRIEND AND GIRLFRIEND, WHO LIVE HERE, START ARGUING AGAIN. OUT POPS THE MOUSE INTO THE KITCHEN, SQUEAKING HEROICALLY: "STOP, OH STOP! SHE HAS SUCH WONDERFUL BIG BLUE EYES, HE HAS SPECIAL EXTRAVITALITY AND GREAT SPIRIT! SO MAKE PEACE AT ONCE!"

THESE
WORDS ARE
THE PRODUCT
OF MANGA
READING.

THE QUARRELING COUPLE BLINK
DOWN AT THE PROUD, IDEALISTIC
MOUSE. THE GIRLFRIEND SHRIEKS.
THE BOYFRIEND GRABS A BROOM
AND, WILDLY WHACKING, DRIVES THE
MOUSE AROUND THE KITCHEN, BACK
INTO ITS HOLE. "SICK LITTLE VERMIN!"
THE BOYFRIEND BELLOWS,
SLAMMING WITH THE BROOM.

THE POOR MOUSE CRINGES THERE IN ITS LITTLE OUTFIT,
QUAKING. ITS HEROIC DREAMS OF ROMANTIC GOOD-DOING
ARE VICIOUSLY SHATTERED. IT HEARS THE OTHER MICE
SNICKERING IN THE DARKNESS. AND ITS HEART TURNS BLACK
AND BITTER. "VERY WELL!" IT THINKS. "I TRIED TO BRING HOPE
AND HARMONY TO THE SEXES, LOOK WHAT HAPPENED. FROM
NOW ON I WILL BE BITTERMOUSE—MANGA-STYLE ANTIHERO
OF ROMANTIC DISCORD AND DISTRESS!"

THE MOUSE EMBARKS ON ITS NEW, EVIL CRUSADE;
AND OBVIOUSLY, LOOKING AROUND, WE SEE IT'S
MUCH BETTER AT THINGS THIS TIME.

Tanya suffers from a terrible, embarrassing secret. She longs to share it but dares not. (You know the feeling.) Finally in desperation she writes the secret in tiny letters on a scrap of paper. She makes her best friend Teresa swear not to tell a soul! Then she thrusts the paper into bewildered Teresa's hand and runs from the room. Teresa opens the paper, reads its dreadful secret, turns scarlet with shame, and tears it up.

Now she has a secret burning like acid into her peace of mind. But she's promised not to tell a soul! However, strictly speaking, can't she *write* the secret, as it was written to her? And Teresa

does so, on a scrap of paper, with the plea that
the reader not tell a soul what he or she has
learned! And please tear the paper up! She leaves
it on a bus seat and dashes out through the
doors.

A guy picks up the scribbled paper, yawns,
reads, bursts out laughing—and then turns red
with shame. Now he has the awful secret. It eats
away at him. And though he's a perfect stranger
to whomever was the writer, he's honorable. He's
dying to tell a buddy; but he mustn't! But can't
he do what the note writer did? And he does, he
leaves his version of the scribbled secret and its
no-tell plea on a bench in the park, and dashes
off through the greenery.

In this way, on and on the secret travels
around town. Until one day, of course, it arrives
back in Tanya's very own hands. And her hands
tremble as she reads, and her heart leaps in des-
perate secret joy that, unbelievably, she's not the
only one? Oh sweetest joy, she's not the only one!

The Nasty News

SOLSTICE

Brad and Denise's first date is also their last!

It's morning. A father blearily tastes his coffee and props up the newspaper for a look. The main headline announces a date of seasonal significance: June 20. The father's head snaps up. "Spring is over!" he cries, gaping out at the room. He turns immediately into a mass of ice cream.

His wife comes through the door. She rushes up to the great melting bulk of dreamy-creamy vanilla, formerly her husband. Her eye falls on the newspaper headline. She sways and manages a little squeal before toppling over—as a load of refreshing watermelon slices on a serving plate.

The household's two teenagers contribute a colorful beachwear bikini top and an autographed baseball to this seasonal tableau.

Jimmy Murphy plays with his dog—or is it the other way around?!

The mayor's emergency press conference comes to a sudden halt!

Down at public safety headquarters, a burly guy in a trench coat—a crusty veteran of many changing seasons—scowls at the reports coming in from all over the city. "This crazy First Day of S——!" he mutters, careful not to speak the word. "The madness and havoc it causes in people's lives!" And he squints through the window blinds at the sunshine, counting the long disastrous hours to go.■

Woof Woof,
Tweet Tweet

My friend with a bird
Says, "Haven't you heard?

My *winged one*'s just dying
To escape and go flying."

Says I: "Perhaps you should join him."
My friend: "But that'll just spoil him:

He's really no eagle,
In fact he's a *beagle*!

And a dog in midair
Would grow pompous, I fear."

"You're right!" says I then.
"Best lock the mutt/bird in!—

Let it woof woof and tweet tweet—*who cares.*"

♫ Karaoke ♫

A fellow named Fenwick goes to a karaoke bar with his pals. He's a pretty good singer, but tonight, he is simply *awesome*. He glides from one smooth old Frank Sinatra classic to another, and he "nails" each one, as they say. So that when he stumbles back to his seat, dazed, dazzled, he senses the ghosts of legendary Las Vegas crooners rising in their graves to applaud!

His pals shrug, grinning weakly. "Not bad," they grunt.

"'Not bad'?" Fenwick sputters. "Hello? I was just now as good as Sinatra ever was! I could be a star!"

"Aw, come on," they laugh. "Now this guy here: he's good!"

Up on stage some stranger is blaring an inane Barry Manilow tune in a piercing high voice.

"But didn't you *hear* me?" Fenwick protests. "I was . . . *amazing*—I was—"

"Shhhh!" they interrupt. "Have respect for real talent!"

When Barry Manilow–man finishes, applause erupts. Fenwick stares around in disbelief. His disbelief turns to rage when this tuneless nobody is voted Best Performer.

"No! No!" Fenwick cries, making a scene. "Weren't you listening? Didn't you hear and see how great I was?"

But it's no use. And for a while Fenwick's life twists into a nightmare, where a talent blooms astoundingly, and then withers, from the stupidity and cruelty of his friends. They mock his protests and call him a bad sport—and then they banish him from any more karaoke! He pleads with them not to cast him out from the source of his glory. But they refuse!

And that's the end of Fenwick and musical stardom. I wish there was something I could do to rectify this horrible fate, but there isn't. And besides, they're his friends, I didn't pick them!

"Young Love Is Everywhere!"

A girl on the subway smiles. She listens to her music on her headphones. The tune playing now is her favorite, "Young Love Is Everywhere!" by the new all-girl band Blue Poppies. The girl shuts her eyes, and despite being among strangers, she twitches her hips to the infectious rhythm. A guy grins at her, watching from the door. He feels happy, and he twitches his hips too.

An elderly lady looks up from her magazine. "These kids," she thinks, but then she grins. She moves her old hips in her seat. Two schoolboys next to her sneer in embarrassment. Then they hop up and start to twitch.

Shortly the whole subway car is twitching away. The subway train arrives at the next station; many hip-happy folk pour out and take their happiness with them, and it spreads, as happiness will. And in a matter of a moment or two, hips are shaking and twitching in rhythm on the stairs, out into the station, spreading wide through the crowded doors out into the streets. The whole vast busy city is bobbing and swaying to the rhythms of "Young Love Is Everywhere!" by Blue Poppies.

Way down below, the subway car speeds on through the dark tunnels. The girl has her eyes still shut, singing, "Young Love Is Everywhere!" to herself. And so she misses the whole thing. But so what, she's having a fine time anyway.

CHERRY
BLOSSOMS

Celia is on her way to the bus stop. A breeze blows, cool and damp, but the sun is newly toasty. "It's spring!" thinks Celia happily.

Suddenly she feels odd. She stops. She stares down at her hands, her arms. She blinks at them. They're covered with pink blossoms!

"My god," gasps Celia softly. "Just like—"

"*Cherry blossoms!*" shout happy voices.

Out of nowhere a gang of people surge over, throw down a blanket in front of Celia, and commence drinking and laughing and singing.

"How convenient to find a cherry tree flowering right here!" someone whoops gleefully.

Poor Celia, who's very shy, partly because she so spindly and gangly (like a thin tree), gawks at the scene below her. "Please, forgive me, there's some mistake," she stammers.

But only gales of happy laughter greet her announcement.

"I'm sorry, I have to go, to catch the bus," Celia protests meekly, and she starts to edge away.

"Hey, this crazy cherry tree!" someone laughs. "It's *moving*!"

And to many whoops, numerous hands grab Celia around the knees and hold her fast.

"Please, you don't understand!" cries Celia in distress. But the rest of her afternoon, and well on into the evening moonlight, she stands with her long arms outspread as laughter and whooping serenade her.

For a full week afterward, Celia just hides away at home, covered in exfoliation cream. Finally she returns to normal. But for her the word "spring" never regains its original happy meaning, unfortunately.

Purple Earmuffs

If this sentence contains exactly *nineteen* words, your very *least* favorite person will turn into a turtle wearing purple earmuffs!

Sleepy

A writer (like me?) is trying to write. But he's sleepy. He'd much rather sneak a few winks than work. Who wouldn't?

He remembers as a kid getting sleepy while studying at school, and how he'd put his head down on his math book, and close his eyes.

And so he does now, on his laptop. In a couple minutes he's actually snoring.

At this point the horrid little goblin that wandered into the writer's apartment last night wakes up behind the sofa. He blinks his ugly reddened eyes. He hears snores. He peers furtively over the sofa.

"So . . ." he thinks. "A writer, eh? The evil sort of human who's always saying awful things about me and my kind!"

He decides it's payback time. He creeps over to the desk and wiggles up the chair, and whispers a terrible spell into the sleeping writer's ear. The spell will render the writer's mind a complete creative vacuum when he wakes up. He'll never have another clever thought in his head again!

The goblin scrambles out the window, chuckling.

The last past of this evil business has been witnessed by the writer's guardian angel coming out of the bathroom. He's invisible, of course. "Oh gosh, oh gosh," he thinks. "Got a lot of work here, to straighten all of this out!"

Then he yawns. He's sleepy too. He'd much rather nap than work right now. And he tiptoes away into the writer's bedroom and lies down, promising just to shut his eyes for five nice minutes, at most.

But you know how it goes when you're sleepy.

So the poor writer wakes up, unprotected. And the terrible spell takes hold, as of course you can tell from this story.

Anya von Bremzen

Writer-performer Barry Yourgrau wrote *NASTYbook*, a bunch of twisted stories. Next came *Another NASTYbook: The Curse of the Tweeties*, a demented novel that's nuts about candy bars and *manga*. Barry has a history of startling performances—on MTV and NPR, and even in a rock music video he starred in! Kids all over scream and laugh and gulp whenever Barry reads aloud at their schools. He won a Drama-Logue Award for performing his book *Wearing Dad's Head*. He's also acted in Hollywood films—as a bee-stung high school principal and a scary-scary scientist.

Born in South Africa, Barry came to the U.S. as a boy . . . a *very strange* boy. Keep up to date on all his NASTY mischief—check out www.nastybook.com and Barry's own website, www.yourgrau.com. And listen to his *NASTYbook* audiobook.

Nice is overrated!

"Very funny . . . and magnificently nasty."
—Neil Gaiman (author of *Coraline*)

"Deliciously macabre."
—*Kirkus Reviews*

"Perfectly wonderful."
—Booksense.com

"An up-to-date twist."
—*NPR Weekend Edition Sunday*

"Gruesome."
—*Publishers Weekly*

"Devious."
—ALA *Booklist*

"Wickedly fun to read."
—*Time Out New York Kids*

The NASTY World
of Barry Yourgrau